Donkey Disaster

Peter Clover

ILLUSTRATED BY

Carolyn Dinan

OXFORD
UNIVERSITY PRESS

to Bryan with love and affection

OXFORD
UNIVERSITY PRESS

Great Clarendon Street, Oxford OX2 6DP

Oxford University Press is a department of the University of Oxford.
It furthers the University's objective of excellence in research, scholarship,
and education by publishing worldwide in

Oxford New York

Athens Auckland Bangkok Bogotá Buenos Aires
Cape Town Chennai Dar es Salaam Delhi Florence Hong Kong Istanbul
Karachi Kolkata Kuala Lumpur Madrid Melbourne Mexico City Mumbai
Nairobi Paris São Paulo Shanghai Singapore Taipei Tokyo Toronto Warsaw

with associated companies in Berlin Ibadan

Oxford is a registered trade mark of Oxford University Press
in the UK and in certain other countries

British Library Cataloguing in Publication Data available

ISBN 0-19-275123-9

1 3 5 7 9 10 8 6 4 2

Designed and Typeset by Mike Brain Graphic Design Limited, Oxford

Printed in Great Britain by Cox & Wyman Ltd, Reading, Berkshire

Whistlewind Farm is a fictional donkey sanctuary and the practises described, although authentic,
are not based on those used by any real donkey sanctuary.

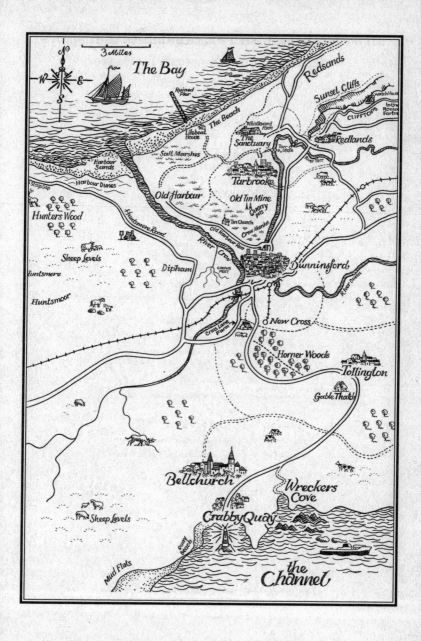

OTHER BOOKS IN THE SERIES

Donkey Danger
Donkey Drama

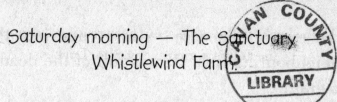

Saturday morning — The Sanctuary —
Whistlewind Farm.

'Keep those tapes nice and taut!' called Jenny Lester on her way back to the farmhouse. Danni looked up across the paddock fencing and pulled a grunge face.

'We know,' she grinned. 'We've done it hundreds of times, haven't we, Tim?'

Danni and her best friend Tim Bentley were working in the home field, marking and taping a safe pasture for the donkeys to graze in. The whole field had to be checked and cleared of ragwort before any donkeys could be allowed in. They taped and cleared sections systematically. Ragwort was a dangerous weed — a deadly poison to donkeys if eaten by mistake.

Peter Lester, Danni's father, had spotted the dreaded R with his eagle eyes when he was checking the boundary fence for gaps and broken rails. The last thing they wanted at The Sanctuary was for any of their donkeys — especially Houdini who could squeeze through

1

the eye of a needle — to escape into the neighbouring field. It was full of the deadly ragwort.

'It's a pity we don't have that corner field,' said Danni. 'We could easily clear it and put it to good use. With new donkeys coming all the time, a big field like that would be brilliant.'

'No one ever uses it, do they,' stated Tim. 'Who does it belong to, anyway?'

Danni pulled the tape taut between the two posts and secured it with a nylon flexi-tie. 'I don't know,' she answered. 'But I bet Mum does. You make a start on the next section while I go and ask. I'll grab two Cokes while I'm at it!'

Then she raced off with her wild, dark hair in a ponytail, whipping the air. It almost cracked like a whip.

Whistlewind Farm had been bought for a song at auction only six months ago, and became the Lesters' lifelong dream — a donkey retreat devoted to providing loving care to rescued and unwanted donkeys.

The Sanctuary had eighteen residents now — the Lesters liked to call their donkeys 'residents' — and they were hoping to expand and offer homes to many more. But the problem was space. They desperately needed more grazing pastures. And suddenly Danni thought she had the simple answer. But things were never that simple.

The farmhouse kitchen

Jenny Lester didn't know who the corner field actually belonged to. Peter Lester seemed to think it was once part of the Whistlewind estate.

'I'm sure it was mentioned somewhere in the deeds when we bought this place,' he said. 'Along with that workman's cottage up the lane.'

'That was a long time ago,' agreed Jenny, 'when *all* the fields and surrounding meadows belonged to the Whistlewind family. I expect it's been sold many times since then.'

'I wonder what happened to the Whistlewinds?' pondered Danni.

'They all moved away, I suppose,' suggested Peter.

'Gradually sold off their land, I guess. Acre by acre, plot by plot. Until over the years it all disappeared.'

'The Whistlewinds have gone, but we're still here!' chirped Danni. 'And so is their farm — in name only!'

Jenny smiled. 'But it's not half the size it used to be.'

'It will be again,' interrupted Danni. 'Once we find out who owns Corner field and buy it from them.'

Jenny laughed; even though she liked the

idea, she knew it wasn't that simple.

'Fields cost money,' she said.

'Money we don't have,' echoed Dad.

'Then we'll just have to think of a way to raise some,' exclaimed Danni. 'I'll put Tim on the case. His ideas are always brill.' Then she grabbed two Cokes from the fridge and went back outside to check on Tim's taping.

The home field

Danni and Tim stared into the neighbouring field. Their arms dangled lazily over the top rail of the wooden fence.

'It's at least three acres,' guessed Danni. She took a sip from her can.

'That's a lot of field,' agreed Tim. He ran a hand across his blond crop and twiddled with the long gelled bit at the front. He always did that when he was thinking.

'Bed and breakfast breaks!' he announced.

Danni curled up her top lip and groaned.

5

She didn't seem to like the idea one bit. 'It's a bit ordinary, isn't it? Lots of people do B and B round here.'

'Ah! But there's a twist,' grinned Tim. He finished his Coke in one glug. 'We offer holiday breaks with a difference — an opportunity to experience close working contact with donkeys. House guests come and pay for their keep, and get to help out at the same time.'

'You mean they pay to come here and work!' laughed Danni.

'Sort of,' he grinned. 'Only they *do* get to be with all the donkeys. So there is a bonus!'

'I like it,' said Danni. 'I think it's brilliant. And Mum'll love it too. I can't wait to tell her.'

'I suppose we could clear out the two back bedrooms.' Jenny was already making plans.

'A quick lick of paint,' suggested Peter. 'Make the rooms cosy. Nice farmhouse breakfasts. You know, this *could* work.'

'Let's do it, then.' Jenny was really keen to

get started. 'We'll place a few ads and see what response we get.'

Saturday morning — one week later

'A booking! We've got our first booking.' Jenny burst into the kitchen waving a notepad across the table.

'Who's it from?' Danni was just as excited as her mum.

'Mrs Springer and her daughter Robyn,' said Jenny. 'It was the daughter who phoned

7

and made a six-day booking. She sounded really nice. It's to be a birthday surprise for her mother. And they're arriving on Friday.'

'Well, the rooms are ready,' announced Peter, 'so it's all systems go!'

'What will we get them to do?' asked Danni. 'Everything!' she grinned cheekily.

Jenny smiled. 'There are eighteen residents out there who need looking after. And they're all big on TLC.'

'TLC?' quizzed Danni.

'Tender, loving care. We can't expect the guests to do any of the mucky stuff,' said Jenny. 'Just lots of hands on care and attention.'

'They could clear ragwort,' suggested Danni.

But Jenny wasn't so sure. Ragwort had to be pulled up by the root and burnt. If it was just pulled and left in the paddock, donkeys might easily eat it by mistake. And a little ragwort eaten over a long period was just as deadly as a lot taken in one go. No, Jenny wasn't too keen on *that* idea.

'I thought we could assign each guest three

8

or four donkeys to look after. Give them charts on clipboards and get them to perform the daily routine health checks.' Jenny had worked this out the night before. 'The guest could then choose one donkey as a special project and be entirely responsible for "that resident" during their stay with us.'

'They could have grooming lessons,' suggested Danni. She was beginning to get the idea now.

'And they could monitor their grazing and have an exercise regime,' said Tim.

'It's beginning to sound like a health club,' smiled Peter.

Little did he know, someone else was having exactly those same thoughts.

Buddleia Villa — Arlinton — Friday morning

'The Sanctuary,' chirped Mrs Springer. 'What a lovely birthday surprise!'

Robyn smiled and gave her mother a hug.

'Six whole days at a health farm,' beamed Mrs Springer. 'I'd better go and pack.'

Robyn had never said it was a health farm. Robyn knew that she should own up. She knew she should tell her mother that The Sanctuary was a donkey retreat. But she also knew that if she did, then mother wouldn't go. And Robyn so desperately wanted to. She loved animals. Especially donkeys. And she was looking forward to this holiday at The Sanctuary more than anything. Half term was always boring at Buddleia Villa. School had broken up and this was a perfect opportunity for Mrs Springer to realize that *she* loved donkeys too. Even though she didn't know it yet.

The Sanctuary — Whistlewind Farm — the same Friday morning

While most of the other residents were grazing peacefully, Danni was in the home field playing football with Shadow. Danni kicked the ball as

hard as she could and the little black racing
donkey charged after it like a dynamo.

'Come on, Shadow,' called Danni. 'Bring it
back like a good donkey.'

Shadow loved this game and dribbled the
ball back across the grassy pasture.

The other donkeys stood around watching in
amazement, ears tick-tocking from side to side
as their mouths chewed the fresh green shoots
of grass.

Suddenly, Shadow stopped midfield. He
threw up his woolly head and let rip with his
unique, ear-piercing bray. Hee — Hawww!! It

was awesome! Not only was Shadow the family pet, he was also The Sanctuary guard donkey.

The little black fellow had seen two men crossing the Corner field, directly behind Danni, and sent out an alarm.

Danni spun around to check out the cause of Shadow's warning. Two workmen were walking into the adjoining field. They carried striped poles and some kind of equipment stored in metal boxes.

They paused for a moment and glanced over to The Sanctuary, then carried on with their business. The other donkeys became very curious. They lined themselves up along the paddock fencing which separated the two fields and rested their fuzzy chins on the top rail.

Eighteen pairs of eyes locked on to the two strangers in their midst. A low bray rumbled in their throats.

Danni, too, watched with equal interest as the workmen staked several poles, at strategic points, around the field. Then, with a funny piece of equipment resembling a telescope on a tripod, they studied the striped poles and wrote down notes on their clipboards.

'What on earth are they doing! And what's that "thing" they're looking through?' As usual, Danni was thinking out loud. But Shadow was listening. His ears twitched. Jenny was listening too as she walked up to the fence.

'That's a theodolite,' she said calmly. 'They're using it to measure the ground level of the field.'

'Why would anyone want to measure the ground level of a field?' asked Danni.

'It's usually building contractors,' answered Jenny. 'They measure the levels to see if the land is suitable for developing! You stay here,' she said, then hopped over the fence and went over to talk with the workmen.

13

It turned out that the men were working for Agrocure Universal Developments. They were assessing the potential of the field. AUD wanted to develop the plot and build a laboratory for testing agricultural insecticides and herbicides. In other words they wanted to build a chemical factory unit.

Later that same morning — the farmhouse kitchen

'A factory! It can't possibly happen. I don't believe it!!' Peter Lester was gobsmacked. 'How could the council planning department allow a factory to be built in the middle of the countryside. It's unthinkable!'

'I know,' admitted Jenny. 'I can't believe it either. I'd better go into Tarbrooke and find out what's going on.' She pulled her quilted jacket from the hook behind the kitchen door and went out to the Range Rover.

Shadow came trotting over to see Jenny and

pushed his nose after her through the open car door. Jenny rubbed his muzzle. 'Sorry, boy. I'm in a hurry.'

Tarbrooke

Twenty minutes later she was in the council offices behind the Town Hall, talking with a clerk.

A thin, poker-faced man with bulbous eyes and dark greasy hair sat across the desk from her. He looked a bit like a fish. His name was Mr Perch. He answered all of Jenny's questions as best he could. In fact, Mr Perch was a mine of information.

Agrocure Universal Developments had made an application to the Department of Agriculture for permission to install a chemical factory unit in the Corner field. The application was being considered.

'The factory is offering a public service by producing and testing chemicals to improve pest control and aid crop protection,' gulped Mr Perch. His mouth opened and closed like a goldfish when he spoke. 'The countryside is the ideal location for such a factory,' he concluded.

'But it's almost on top of my donkey sanctuary,' complained Jenny. 'What if they start spraying and testing in the fields? What about my donkeys? Some of them have breathing problems. The Corner field could be put to so much better use by The Sanctuary. We don't need chemical factories in Tarbrooke.' Jenny sounded really angry.

Mr Perch assured Jenny that there would be strict regulations enforced, controlling any spraying outside the unit. But added that if she disapproved, she should write directly to the Ministry of Agriculture.

'Who owns the Corner field anyway?' asked Jenny.

16

Mr Perch told her that it was one of the two remaining plots belonging to the Whistlewind estate.

'It belongs to distant relatives now living in the North of England,' he said. 'They've decided to sell both plots at auction.'

'At auction!' exclaimed Jenny excitedly. 'So the field hasn't been sold yet!' A glimmer of hope lit up her face. She breathed a sigh of relief.

'The auction is this coming Monday,' added Mr Perch with a raised eyebrow. 'In the reading room at the Town Hall.'

'This coming Monday,' gasped Jenny. Now her disappointment felt worse than ever.

Back in the Kitchen — Whistlewind Farm

'This coming Monday!' repeated Peter Lester. Everyone was sitting around the kitchen table cradling mugs of hot tea. 'That's just after the weekend. Three days away. What chance have we got to raise enough money to buy a whole field in three days! Our first B and B guests are arriving today and their bill will just about cover the cost of painting and fixing up the rooms.'

It was true. Even if the B and B idea was really successful and took off like a rocket, it could take months before they could even think of trying to buy the field. It seemed totally useless.

'I can't imagine a whacking great factory unit in the Corner field,' moaned Danni. 'It's horrible. I bet it stinks!'

'I can't believe it's actually going to happen,' said Jenny in amazement.

'Maybe it won't,' piped up Tim, trying to sound positive and cheerful. 'Perhaps we can raise the money some other way!'

'How?' three voices asked together.

'I don't know, yet,' squirmed Tim. Suddenly he felt a right dork for suggesting the very idea. 'It's just that it's not like The Sanctuary to give up!'

'We're not giving up!' boomed Jenny. 'There's just nothing we can do, that's all.'

'What we need is a miracle,' sighed Danni. 'A big fat miracle.'

Brooke Bridge

A white Mercedes crossed the stone pack-horse bridge and purred along the narrow country lane. Robyn Springer sank back into the plush leather seat and shot a sideways glance at her mother.

Robyn Springer was twelve. Mrs Springer settled for being forty. She'd been forty for ages now. She was forty again this year and The Sanctuary was her special birthday treat.

Mrs Springer was looking forward to spending a whole week at a health farm. It was something she'd always dreamed of doing. Robyn wasn't looking forward to telling her mother that they were heading for a donkey retreat. So she decided not to tell her. Mrs Springer was going to find out for herself very soon anyway.

Some surprises are best left to the last minute.

The Sanctuary

'Guess what's just pulling up in the drive?' Danni's eyes were almost popping out of her head as she dashed into the farmhouse.

'A car,' teased Peter, 'or maybe a stampeding herd of African elephants!' He was poring over The Sanctuary's accounts trying to think of things to sell and ways to save money. Money to buy the Corner field.

'Yes, it *is* a car, clever clogs,' Danni joked in return. 'But it's some car. You've just gotta see it.'

'It must be our house guests — the Springers,' said Jenny. She pulled the curtain aside and peered into the farmyard.

'It's a white Mercedes,' gawped Jenny as the flashy car slid to a silent halt outside their door.

'I think the Queen has just arrived,' laughed Danni.

Inside the car, Mrs Springer smiled. 'How quaint.'

She studied the polished wooden sign, posted outside in the cobbled yard — 'The Sanctuary,' she read. Then turned to Robyn. 'Thank you, darling. It's the best birthday surprise I've ever had.'

Jenny was wearing a white doctor's coat when she greeted the house guests and led them through the entrance hall and off up the stairs to their adjoining rooms. Jenny thought the white coat looked very professional. She thought it gave The Sanctuary a clean, clinical image. She particularly wanted to portray a wholesome, sterile environment — in case any of the guests were worried about health regulations or catching anything from the donkeys. Especially Mr Barnaby and Dolores who were still a bit flea bitten and daggy looking from lice infestation. Both residents had been terribly neglected by their previous owner. They were doing fine now at The Sanctuary, but they still looked a bit rough around the edges. And it could put some people off.

Jenny thought the white coat made her look like a vet. Someone who would know everything there was to know about donkeys. That would create the perfect first impression. Peter thought it made her look like a dental hygienist. Mrs Springer thought she was one of the beauticians.

'When will you tell us about the schedules?' asked Mrs Springer brightly. She pressed the palm of her hand down on the bedding, testing the mattress. Mrs Springer thought the room was a little spartan but it was Robyn's treat so she didn't say anything.

'Perhaps you'd like to settle in first,' suggested Jenny. 'Then I'll give you a tour of The Sanctuary and introduce you to all our residents!'

'That will be nice,' smiled Mrs Springer. She patted her apricot coloured hair. 'I shall look forward to that.'

Robyn couldn't help giggling, even though she had butterflies the size of sparrows fluttering in her stomach.

When they had unpacked and freshened up, Robyn and her mother went downstairs and wandered into the lounge.

Before the tour, Jenny gave them a little pep-talk. Danni and Tim were trying to peek at the guests through a crack in the lounge door. They thought Robyn looked cool. She had really long, silky blonde hair, pulled back with neat little butterfly grips. Her clothes were cool too. Pedal pushers and designer T-shirt.

Jenny began, 'The first residents we shall meet will be Mr Barnaby and Dolores, out in the recovery barn.' Mrs Springer looked startled.

Jenny continued, 'Now I don't want you to be concerned about their condition. We've bandaged their legs to stop them from nipping and biting their sores. But it's not as bad as it looks. They are receiving the finest treatment here at The Sanctuary.'

Mrs Springer shot a glance towards Robyn. She couldn't help thinking, What kind of a place is this? Residents biting their legs!

It didn't take long after that for Mrs Springer to realize that The Sanctuary wasn't a health farm after all. Each resident she was introduced to had a furry face and long waggling ears. The schedules included health checks, teeth and hoof inspection, and involved grooming and general donkey care. There was no mention of massage treatments, herbal steam baths, seaweed wraps, or beauty therapies of any kind.

Mrs Springer was really cool about it. She wasn't happy — she was cool. She looked really livid at first but she was a good sport at heart.

It was quite obvious to her that Robyn wanted this experience of working with donkeys.

Mrs Springer seemed happy enough to indulge her daughter. But she couldn't help giving off a feeling that it was all a bit too menial and mucky for her.

Jenny assigned Ethel, Blue, Dixie, and Daisy to Mrs Springer. Mrs Springer chose Blue as her special project. She thought Blue looked less trouble than the other three. The donkey was half asleep on his feet, dozing in the warm sunshine.

Robyn was assigned Jasper, Houdini, Rosie, and Poppy. She chose Houdini as her special project. Houdini was a tricky character famed for his numerous escapes. Hardly a week went by without Houdini finding some gap, fence, gate, or barrier to squeeze, wriggle, or burst through. Robyn couldn't wait to get started. Mrs Springer couldn't wait to go home. She went up to her room to have a lie down and rest her eyes. Birthdays can be very tiring.

Outside in the farmyard

'Hi! I'm Danni and this is Tim.' Robyn beamed them both a huge smile.

'Your mother doesn't want to be here, does she?' winked Tim.

Robyn shook her head. She didn't mind being asked.

'Mother wouldn't have come if she'd known it was a donkey sanctuary,' admitted Robyn. 'She sort of assumed that The Sanctuary was a health farm, so I just let her believe it *was*.'

Danni and Tim thought that was a great laugh!

'Mother even thought that *your* mother was a health and beauty therapist,' added Robyn.

26

Danni creased up.

'But she is,' laughed Tim. 'She's an expert on donkeys' health and welfare. And all her 'residents' *are* beautiful.'

Danni agreed with that and gave Tim a slap on the back. 'Come on, Robyn,' she said. 'We'll show you how to muck out a stable.'

Tarbrooke — later that afternoon

Jenny Lester posted a notice in the local supermarket. It was all about AUD — Agrocure Universal Developments. The poster was asking local residents if they knew of the factory's development plans. There was also a petition to sign. Jenny couldn't stop AUD buying the Corner field, but she could certainly protest and try to prevent the experimental testing site from being built. The more people who knew about it the better.

As she came out of the supermarket, Jenny bumped into Mrs Springer.

'Just thought I'd check out the shops,' she said, looking a little guilty and embarrassed. 'I mean, it's not compulsory is it? Cleaning out the stables and everything. Robyn loves it but I'm more of an organizer than the hands-on type.'

Jenny smiled. 'You don't have to worry, Mrs Springer. The Sanctuary is for you to enjoy in whatever way you please. You don't have to do anything you don't want to.'

'It's not that I'm lazy,' insisted Mrs Springer, gazing fixedly at her long, polished fingernails.

Jenny chatted and explained why they were doing the bed and breakfast breaks. She told Mrs Springer in detail about the field. About AUD. And about her concerns over the production and testing of herbicides and pesticides so close to The Sanctuary.

'Maybe I can help,' offered Mrs Springer. 'I used to run my own business before I retired. Campaigns were my speciality. I'll get names on that petition. You just leave it to me!'

Jenny couldn't help smiling.

'And don't worry. I won't shirk my

responsibilities at The Sanctuary,' she added, tottering into the supermarket on extremely high heels.

The Sanctuary — Whistlewind Farm

Danni, Tim, and Robyn had mucked out two stables. Danni was now running through the standard health checks which they performed daily on every single Sanctuary donkey while grooming.

'The first thing to look for,' began Danni, 'is the donkey's attitude when you approach. A healthy donkey should be alert, and standing with its ears pricked.'

Houdini immediately stood to attention when he saw them coming.

Danni clipped the lead rope to Houdini's head collar and tethered the donkey to a ring in the farmyard wall. Robyn watched keenly and made notes on her clipboard.

'Grooming doesn't just make the donkeys

look smarter,' said Danni. 'It also improves their circulation.'

'And you get to check them over at the same time,' added Tim, eager to show off to Robyn that he knew about donkeys, too!

Danni showed Robyn how to check the donkey's face, eyes, nose, and mouth. How to feel their legs and joints for swelling, bumps, or small wounds.

Then Tim showed her how to clean out the donkeys' hoofs with a hoof pick.

Houdini was brilliant, so Danni rewarded him with his favourite titbit. A gingernut biscuit.

'Now you have a go,' said Danni.

It wasn't quite as simple as it looked. Robyn tried her best, but somehow Houdini managed to free himself from his lead rope and trotted off across the yard to play football with Shadow.

'I can see I've got a lot to learn,' grinned Robyn. She blew her fringe out of her eyes and made more notes on the clipboard.

'Each donkey is different,' said Tim. 'Through grooming you'll gradually get to know their individual characteristics and learn all about their funny little ways.'

'We'll have another go later,' said Danni. 'But first, let's have some fun!'

They took Houdini and Shadow into the field to have a kick-around. Robyn had never seen donkeys playing football before. It was brilliant.

Later that afternoon — around 3p.m.

When Mrs Springer finally returned from the shops, she went to The Sanctuary office and handed Jenny a pile of flyers.

'I've had these run off for you,' she said. 'I found a little office supply shop with a

31

photocopier. Don't worry,' she added, seeing Jenny's eyes widen at the size of the paper stack. 'It won't cost you a thing. My treat.'

Jenny was relieved.

'I've already given a pile to the newsagents who promised to deliver them with tomorrow's newspapers. And I've popped some into the post office for the postman to take on his rounds. Either way, everyone in Tarbrooke will now get to hear of this proposed factory site. And they'll be given the opportunity to sign your petition!' she finished with a satisfied grin.

Now Jenny was impressed.

'I also thought an article in the local paper might help.' Mrs Springer seemed to have found a cause and was giving it her all. 'I've drafted out a rough article. If you've got a PC I could use, I'd be more than happy to type it for you.' Mrs Springer was smiling. She hadn't had so much fun in years.

Jenny was really grateful. It took a lot to run The Sanctuary, and its success relied on the charitable efforts of others.

Mrs Springer plonked herself down in front of the computer while Jenny made her a cup of tea.

The Sanctuary — early Saturday morning

The response from the flyers was amazing. The Sanctuary received two copies. One with their newspaper and one with the post. The letter which accompanied it was from the Ministry of Agriculture acknowledging Jenny's complaint.

Then the phone started ringing. And wouldn't stop. It rang all morning. The calls were from locals who had received the flyers. They were phoning The Sanctuary to offer their support. It gave Jenny new hope to know that the people of Tarbrooke were behind her. But not everyone was against the idea.

That afternoon, The Sanctuary received a visit from Mr Pritchard. Mr Pritchard was one of the workmen Danni had seen measuring the levels of the Corner field. Mr Pritchard was a builder from Huntsmere.

Danni, Tim, and Robyn were sorting out the feeds. They were filling the mangers with barley straw when Mr Pritchard marched into the farmyard. They could hear his loud voice from inside the stables. Mr Pritchard was arguing with Jenny.

'I need this project,' he was saying. 'Building this factory will stop my business from going under. Work's been pretty hard to find lately. And I don't want anyone spoiling things.'

Jenny didn't like being shouted at. She was sympathetic about Mr Pritchard's business problems, but she still didn't want a factory unit on her doorstep. Jenny didn't shout. She spoke very loudly.

Mr Pritchard tore up a flyer in front of Jenny and threw the pieces on the floor. Then he warned her to stop interfering, and stormed off.

Jenny watched him march into the Corner field where he unrolled a big blueprint plan and started taking more measurements.

'What a rude man!' exclaimed Mrs Springer as she stepped out of a barn into the sunlit farmyard. She was leading Blue by his headcollar. 'These donkeys have more manners than that oaf!'

Blue waggled his ears and pushed his soft muzzle into Mrs Springer's arm.

'Isn't that right, Blue?' The old donkey blinked and looked up at her adoringly.

Danni nudged Robyn. 'I think your mother's having a change of heart,' she whispered.

'You're so gentle, aren't you, my darling,' cooed Mrs Springer. She tickled Blue's whiskery chin. 'Not like that nasty man over there. Wait until he reads the newspaper article on Monday,' added Mrs Springer. 'That will give him something to get wild over.'

Saturday afternoon

Throughout the afternoon there were a number of visitors who came to The Sanctuary. Saturdays often brought holidaymakers who wanted to see the donkeys. But today there were local visitors who had seen the flyers, signed the petition, and come to support The Sanctuary in person.

It was only after the last visitor had gone and the 'residents' were being settled down for the evening, that they noticed one of the donkeys was missing. It was Houdini. Robyn felt really awful because she was supposed to be looking after him. Houdini was her special project.

'With all the coming and going today, some visitors must have left a gate open,' said Jenny. 'I'll take the Ranger Rover out and see if I can find him. It's not the first time he's done this!'

'I'll take my car out, too,' said Mrs Springer. 'Two pairs of eyes are better than one.'

'And four eyes are better than two,' said Robyn to her mother. 'I'm coming with you.'

Jenny and Mrs Springer drove around for hours but there was no sign of Houdini.

Danni held the fort at The Sanctuary while Peter went down to Sunset Cliffs and walked the length of Redsands. But there was no Houdini to be found there either.

And by the time Jenny returned it was already starting to get dark. Houdini was well and truly missing.

'There's not much more we can do tonight,' said Peter.

They sat down to supper, but no one really felt like eating anything. Danni pushed her food around with her fork.

'I'll get up really, really early,' she announced, 'and take Shadow out in the fish-cart. We can check out the beach again. *And* the salt marshes.'

'We'll get up early, too,' said Mrs Springer. 'We can take the car out again and all search different areas.'

'He can't have gone that far,' said Jenny confidently. 'Knowing Houdini, he's probably hiding somewhere quite nearby.'

But the following morning there was a phone call from some lads, reporting a donkey trapped in a deep pit out at the quarries by the old tin mine.

Sunday morning — The Sanctuary

Peter Lester took the call. He'd remained at The Sanctuary while the others went off on their separate search parties.

The first thing Peter did was to phone Jenny on her mobile. He couldn't leave The Sanctuary unmanned, but he needed to get to the quarry with the pick-up truck. The truck was fitted with a small crane and winch. They'd need that to get Houdini out of the pit.

After trying several times, he eventually got through to Jenny.

Jenny gave Mrs Springer a ring and asked if

she would donkey-sit back at The Sanctuary while Peter raced to the quarry with the truck.

She was there within minutes. The white Mercedes screamed up the drive and screeched to a halt in the cobbled yard. Robyn leapt out. Peter began to drive away. It was like a relay race.

'Stop,' she yelled. 'I'm coming with you.'

Peter slowed down to let Robyn climb aboard. Then they were gone, leaving Mrs Springer in charge of The Sanctuary.

Redsands

Danni and Tim were heading back to The Sanctuary from the beach when they saw Peter and Robyn in the pick-up truck storming up the road. They quickly put two and two together and guessed that something was up.

Danni flicked the reins across Shadow's back. The little black racing donkey knew and loved that signal. It meant he could gallop mega speed — his favourite pace. Top gear! The little black rocket shot off in pursuit of the pick-up truck.

The Quarry Pits at the Old Tin Mine

The lads who had raised the alert were waiting by the derelict towers at the entrance to the old tin mine. Strictly speaking, the whole locality was declared a hazardous area. The sealed-off tunnels and shafts were unsafe and dangerous, but youths often came to search the quarry pits for fossils.

The last thing they had expected to find was a stray donkey stranded in an old pit.

Jenny was the first to arrive. She parked the Range Rover and followed the boys through a maze of pathways to the top of the pit. A scree of loose stones crunched underfoot as she climbed the gentle slope to the shoulder of the quarry. Patches of green grass survived the rocky terrain.

'What on earth was Houdini thinking of coming all the way out here,' thought Jenny out loud.

She stood perched on the lip of the rocky quarry and peered over the edge.

A pathetic braying rose from its depths, down where bushes and gorse grew in the belly of the pit. Jenny gasped and sucked in her breath, more from relief than shock. The donkey trapped in the pit was a dusty, rusty tan colour. It wasn't Houdini at all. Houdini was pale grey.

The poor donkey looked up at all the faces peering down at it and blew a soft whicker. Its ears were perky and alert as it listened to Jenny's voice. That was a good sign. And the donkey was standing squarely on all fours. That was a miracle. It was a good seven metres drop to the bottom.

41

Minutes later Peter and Robyn arrived in the pick-up truck. Robyn jumped out and scrambled to the top of the quarry. Peter put the truck into low gear and tackled the slope. The truck's thick tyres gripped the shingle track as it crunched and lurched its way to the top. There was a flat platform surface to one side of the quarry where the pit diggers would have once worked from. Peter parked up the truck and pushed two big rocks behind the rear tyres. Then he joined Jenny, Robyn, and the group of lads at the edge, looking down at the rust coloured donkey.

Suddenly, out of the blue, there was an almighty 'Hee-Hawww!' as Shadow raced in

from the downs. The little black racing donkey was famous for his ear shattering braying.

Everyone standing at the pit spun around. Even the stranded donkey pricked up its long pointed ears and looked up to the sky.

Even travelling at top speed Shadow's fish-cart couldn't manage the quarry slope.

Danni left Shadow at the base of the rise and raced to the top with Tim.

'What's happening? Is it Houdini? Is he all right?' Her voice was breathless from the climb. Then she peered down into the big hole and saw that it wasn't their Houdini at all.

'Oh, the poor thing. How on earth did it get down there? Is it hurt?'

'It doesn't appear to be,' said Jenny in amazement. 'But we haven't been down to check yet. I expect it's more frightened than anything else.'

'It must have slipped off that ledge,' said Tim. 'I bet it tried to get down to all that greenery at the bottom.' He pointed out a narrow ledge winding its way around the walls from the top of the pit to almost the bottom. 'It's crumbled away at the end,' he said. 'And it's too high for it to get back up on to!'

'Could a donkey really walk along such a narrow ledge?' asked Robyn. She didn't fancy the idea of attempting it herself.

'Oh, yes,' answered Jenny. 'Donkeys are very sure footed. And Tim's right. It probably went down foraging for food.'

'But there was all that grass back on the downs,' said Robyn. 'Why would it want to climb down into a dangerous pit?'

'That's donkeys for you,' smiled Danni. 'They're fussy grazers and those bushes down there probably looked like a nice juicy snack. Better than old grass.'

'Does anyone know who the donkey might belong to?' asked Jenny.

The group of lads shook their heads.

'I think it just lives wild,' said one boy. 'I've seen it around here before.'

'Perhaps it's escaped from somewhere, like Houdini,' suggested Robyn. Suddenly her thoughts were back with the missing Sanctuary donkey.

'Abandoned is more likely,' said Tim. 'Do you want me to shin down and check her over?' he asked Jenny in the same breath.

'No, I'll do it,' said Peter. He tied a rope around his waist attached to the winch on the pick-up, and lowered himself over the edge.

Jenny operated the automatic winch and reeled out the line, dropping Peter gently down to the donkey.

The donkey backed away. Its ears lay flat against its head and its eyes suddenly looked wild.

'I think we might have a bit of a handful here,' he called up to Jenny.

'Try it with a biscuit!' she threw down some gingernuts which she always kept in her jacket pocket. The donkey cocked its head to one side as Peter offered a biscuit on his outstretched palm.

Yes! Just like most donkeys, this one loved gingernuts.

Peter stroked the furry neck. The donkey didn't seem to mind. But when he raised his hand to stroke its face and ears, it tried to nip him.

Peter pulled back and offered another biscuit. Then he stroked its neck again. He moved on to the withers, the back, then the rump. The donkey was female. She didn't complain, but Peter noticed dark weals on her flesh. Old scars indicating that this donkey had been beaten.

He checked her legs and joints. There was no visible swelling. Only a nasty graze to her front forelock just below the knee. Nothing to worry about.

The donkey didn't seem to be in too bad a condition, although her hoofs desperately needed trimming. They were beginning to take on that Turkish slipper look where the horn of the hoof turns upwards at the front. That was something they could deal with later.

The main problem was going to be lifting the poor thing out.

There was a canvas sling in the back of the truck. Peter and Jenny had used it many times before to lift and rescue donkeys out of tricky and dangerous situations. Jenny winched up the rope and attached the sling to its end. Then she lowered it back down into the pit.

Peter let the donkey see and smell the sling before he gently laid it across her back. He left it there for a few moments to let the donkey get used to the feel of it.

Then he tried to slip the sling under her belly, so she could be hoisted up to safety. But the donkey wasn't having it. She didn't like the sling at all and wouldn't let Peter fasten it or buckle the girth strap.

Suddenly the donkey turned wild again and Peter had to pull the sling off her back to calm her down.

'This isn't going to work,' Peter told the others. 'I'll try again, but I think we've got big problems here.'

'You might have to lead her up,' suggested Jenny from above.

Peter looked puzzled.

'Along the ledge! You might have to bring her up along the ledge,' she repeated.

Peter glanced sideways to the spot where the ledge had crumbled away near the bottom of the pit.

'If we could find something to bridge the gap,' he said. 'Something to make a ramp up to the ledge, then I suppose I might be able to persuade her to climb out.'

'That ledge looks very narrow,' said Robyn. She could hardly believe that a donkey would be able to walk along such a path. But if the donkey wouldn't take the sling then it was the only way out.

They tried several more times with the sling, but it was no-go. The airlift to safety wasn't going to happen.

Peter didn't feel too confident about the ledge. He was a tall man, used to walking with giant strides. The ledge was no more than a slight ridge in the rock face. Peter didn't fancy his chances.

'Let me do it,' offered Danni. 'I can lead the donkey up. I'm only small and that ledge is as wide as a motorway for me.' Danni was fearless. The deep drop into the pit didn't bother her at all. But it bothered Jenny. She thought it looked too dangerous.

'We could tie a safety rope around her,' suggested Tim. And that's exactly what they did.

Danni was lowered into the pit where she made friends with the donkey. It didn't take long. Danni was a natural with animals.

She gently stroked the soft, furry face and tickled the long floppy ears. The donkey looked at Danni with trusting eyes and allowed her to slip on a headcollar.

'Come on, girl,' she whispered gently. 'We'll soon have you out of here!'

Peter had taken the tailboard off the back of the truck and created a makeshift ramp up to the ledge. It was quite steep and Jenny wasn't sure the donkey would be able to manage it. But Danni didn't have a problem. She had some gingernut biscuits to help and was ready to give it her best shot.

'Good luck, Danni!' called Robyn.

'You can do it!' grinned Tim.

Danni glanced up to the shoulder of the pit then palmed the donkey a biscuit.

The second gingernut she held in her clenched fist. Danni let the donkey sniff at it. She let her lick her hand. But she kept the biscuit hidden.

'You want it?' asked Danni. 'Then come and get it!' She took hold of the headcollar and urged the donkey to take a run at the ramp. With a clumsy clatter of hoofs the donkey charged up the ramp and landed on the lower ledge.

Danni rewarded her with the biscuit.

'Good girl. Good girl!' She patted the donkey hard on the neck.

The donkey pricked up her ears and nuzzled Danni's pocket for another titbit.

Danni took advantage of the donkey's curiosity and began walking the ledge.

The donkey followed, sniffing and snorting close behind. With gentle coaxing and several gingernuts, they made it to within metres from the top. Then the donkey lost her nerve and refused to go on any further.

No amount of pulling, coaxing, or biscuits made the slightest difference. The donkey wouldn't budge.

Danni peered down into the pit from the ledge. Then drew back sharply against the rock face and gasped. It was a very long way down. Her hand felt for the safety rope around her waist and she breathed a sigh of relief.

Her other hand reached out to touch and comfort the donkey. She stroked its neck gently. The poor thing was trembling from head to hoof.

'What are we going to do?' Danni called up to her parents. But Jenny and Peter were lost for any ideas.

It was Robyn who came up with a suggestion.

'The donkey is obviously frightened and nervous,' said Robyn. 'And all she's got to look at as she gets nearer to the top are lots of strange faces.'

'Thanks a bunch,' said Tim. 'I didn't think we were that strange!'

Robyn explained. 'To a donkey we probably all look a bit strange and scary. Can't we bring Shadow up here and let the poor thing see a real friendly donkey face!'

Everyone thought that was a brilliant idea. Tim raced down the slope to fetch Shadow.

Everyone else cleared away to let the little black donkey get into position. And the moment the other donkey saw Shadow looking over the edge they knew that Robyn's idea was going to work.

Shadow blew a friendly snort and the trapped donkey waggled her ears like a big friendly rabbit. Danni pulled on the headcollar and the donkey happily walked the rest of the way, eager to get to the top, to Shadow and safety.

But the last few steps became hazardous. The donkey was keen to feel solid ground beneath her hoofs. She pushed past Danni in a mad scrabble to breach the rim. And in doing so, knocked Danni clean off the ledge.

Robyn screamed as Danni plunged into the pit. Jenny gasped

53

and Tim opened his mouth to yell, but nothing came out.

Luckily Peter was operating the winch controlling the safety rope. As Danni fell, the winch took the strain and caught her in mid air. It was like flying. Danni was hoisted to safety. Jenny gave her a hug.

'The things some people do for a bit of attention,' grinned Tim.

Danni nudged him hard in the ribs.

'Ouch!'

The Sanctuary — Whistlewind Farm

Mrs Springer had been trying to telephone Jenny and Peter for ages. But she couldn't get a signal through to their mobiles.

Ten minutes after Peter had left in the pick-up, Houdini turned up in the Corner field.

Mrs Springer spotted him when she was checking on all the other 'residents'. She saw him grazing contentedly in the middle of the field and acted quickly. She didn't want him to disappear again.

Mrs Springer found a headcollar in the tack room and climbed the fence into the field. A whole line of donkeys queued up to watch as she walked through the long wind-whipped grass to collect the runaway.

The Lesters were going to have a nice surprise waiting for them when they got back.

It was four o'clock when the convoy of vehicles ambled up the drive into The Sanctuary. Jenny led the way in the Range Rover, followed by Peter and Robyn with the rescued donkey in the back of the truck. And last but not least trotted Shadow with Danni and Tim in the fish-cart.

Houdini was tethered to a ring in the yard when they all arrived. But he didn't look very

happy. In fact Houdini looked very sorry for himself. He was standing with his head low, ears drooped.

That was the very first thing that Jenny noticed about him. Even when she approached him, Houdini didn't perk up to greet her. Instead, his head hung even lower and he blew a pathetic whicker. His whole body drooped.

Jenny was immediately concerned. She left Peter and the others to settle the new donkey into a cosy stable while she examined Houdini. The poor runaway looked really under the weather. His tummy looked bloated and heavy. When Jenny pressed gently with her fingers the donkey moaned with pain. Jenny didn't like it. Jenny didn't like it at all. She called the vet straight away.

Early evening

'It could be colic,' said the vet. 'But I'm more concerned that it might be ragwort poisoning.'

The vet had taken a quick look at the Corner field where Houdini had turned up. It was full of the killer weed, easily recognized by its distinctive curly leaves and small yellow flowers.

He also found some dead ragwort which had been pulled and left near the fence of The Sanctuary paddock. The weed was just as dangerous dead as it was growing.

'That definitely wasn't there this morning,' insisted Jenny.

The vet knew that the Lesters were very particular about the care and welfare of their donkeys. Both Danni and Tim knew only too well the dangers of this plant. They were always extra careful when clearing an area not to leave any behind. And the grazing paddock was always checked every day.

No, this sudden appearance of the weed was a mystery. It seemed that someone had thrown ragwort onto The Sanctuary property. And it didn't take much brainpower to guess who that might be.

'It's that Mr Pritchard!' accused Danni. 'I'll bet you a week's pocket money, it's him.'

'Now don't go jumping to conclusions,' warned Jenny. 'We don't know for certain. And we can't go around saying things like that about people.'

'But it must have been him,' insisted Danni. 'It wasn't there this morning was it? And we've all been away for most of the day.'

Suddenly Mrs Springer looked sheepish. She went to say something. Then decided against it.

'Will Houdini be all right?' asked Robyn.

The vet gave the sick donkey an injection.

'It's hard to tell just yet,' he said. 'We'll have to wait and see how he is in the morning. Hopefully, if it is ragwort poisoning then we've caught it in time.'

Houdini was taken to an isolation stable, where he could rest and be quiet on his own, away from the other donkeys. Jenny and Danni made him as comfortable as they could. Now all they could do was wait.

The new resident

They named the new donkey Lucky. When Danni looked in on her she was a picture of contentment. A cosy stable, plenty of sweet barley straw, and a trough of fresh drinking water. This donkey was obviously used to a hard life. Her arrival at The Sanctuary must have seemed like a step into paradise.

Lucky's ears pricked up when she saw

Danni. The donkey was still nervous of being stroked around the face and ears, but she was quite happy to have her neck patted.

There are so many donkeys out there that need loving, caring homes, thought Danni. She risked trying Lucky with a gentle hug. It made Danni so cross to think that some people could just abandon donkeys. Treat them cruelly and get away with it. They were beautiful, sensitive animals. They needed loving care and attention. And Danni would always be there to give it.

Lucky leaned her weight against Danni, enjoying the close contact of the cuddle. She closed her eyes and rumbled a happy snort.

Danni also looked in on Houdini before she went in for her supper. Houdini still looked very sorry for himself, and barely gave Danni a second glance. She fondled his velvet ears and kissed him on the forehead. Rest, peace, and quiet was what the vet had ordered.

'Please get better, boy,' she whispered. 'Please, please, please get well soon.'

Monday morning — the isolation stable

The next morning found Jenny, Danni, and Robyn standing in the isolation stable, waiting for the vet. Houdini was lying down on a bed of straw. His flanks heaved with each laboured breath he took.

'Oh, Mum. Is he going to be all right?' worried Danni. But Jenny didn't know.

The vet arrived and hurried to the stable. He knelt down next to Houdini and opened his black bag. Then he gave the donkey an injection.

It seemed to help. Within minutes, Houdini's breathing seemed calmer and his eyes flickered open. Danni felt like bursting into tears, but she didn't. She forced herself to be strong. If she was going to work at The Sanctuary and grow up to be a vet, then she had to get used to seeing sick donkeys. But it wasn't easy.

Houdini lay there looking up at everyone. He didn't get up though.

'Is it ragwort poisoning?' asked Jenny finally. The vet wasn't certain.

'It could just as easily be a bad case of colic,' he said.

Danni thought of Mr Pritchard and his precious building project. She was still convinced that he had deliberately tried to poison their donkeys. And she didn't think he should get away with it.

Later that morning — Tarbrooke

The Corner field was going under the auctioneer's hammer at eleven thirty. Although Jenny couldn't afford to put in a bid, she wanted to be there to witness the sale. Mrs Springer had organized a small protest group who were outside the town hall collecting more names for their petition. Jenny carried a placard demanding an immediate ban on any kind of chemical testing in the area. The crowd was making quite a noise.

Suddenly Jenny was confronted by a smart middle aged man in a grey pinstriped suit. His name was James Ditchfield — Managing Director of Agrocure Universal Developments.

'You obviously have no idea how a testing facility like this works, have you?' he asked.

James Ditchfield was smug. Jenny didn't like his attitude at all.

'The Ministry of Agriculture are quite aware of the strict controls and regulation policies we enforce in a project of this kind,' he said. 'So you silly people are just all wasting your time. The project is safe, sound, and sanitized.'

'And selfish,' replied Jenny quickly. 'What about the donkey sanctuary. You don't give a fig about our donkeys, do you? You're just hoping to buy that field for next to nothing. Building your rotten factory. And make lots of money. You can pull the wool over the council's eyes but you can't fool me.'

James Ditchfield looked Jenny straight in the eye, then walked inside the Town Hall building.

Mrs Springer joined Jenny and sat with her at the back of the hall as the auctioneer began.

There were only a handful of bidders there. Not many people were that interested in buying an overgrown field or a tumbledown cottage.

The Corner field was announced separately as lot number one, and the bidding opened at six hundred pounds. James Ditchfield took the lead bid.

'Do I hear seven hundred?' asked the auctioneer. A local man raised his hand.

'Do I hear eight?'

James Ditchfield took the bid.

'Nine hundred,' called another bidder.

'One thousand,' called James Ditchfield.

The hall went very quiet.

Another bid came from the back of the hall.

'One thousand five hundred!' It was Mrs Springer.

'Two thousand,' countered James Ditchfield without looking around.

'Two thousand five hundred,' called Mrs Springer.

'You can't,' whispered Jenny.

'Yes I can,' said Mrs Springer.

'Three thousand,' called James Ditchfield.

'Four,' countered Mrs Springer.

'Stop it,' muttered Jenny. But she wouldn't.

The bidding rose to six thousand pounds with Mrs Springer holding the bid.

'Do I hear seven?' asked the auctioneer. The silence in the hall was deafening. Everyone was looking at the Managing Director of AUD who was staring directly ahead at the auctioneer.

'Going once,' announced the auctioneer. 'Going twice.'

He was about to close the sale to Mrs Springer for six thousand pounds, when James Ditchfield called, 'Ten thousand pounds.'

Hushed gasps filled the air. No way was Jenny going to let Mrs Springer top that. She grabbed her arm and dragged her outside.

'They've won,' said Jenny. 'Let's leave it at that. They've bought the field,' she gave a deep sigh and resigned herself to failure.

'But they haven't got council approval yet!' grinned Mrs Springer. 'I'm going to stick around for a bit. See what I can find out!'

Jenny wanted to get away. She was anxious

to get back to The Sanctuary to see Houdini and her 'residents'. At least she still had her donkeys. And the donkeys still had Jenny.

The Sanctuary — Whistlewind Farm

Danni was waiting for her mum at the top of the drive. She looked as if she had been crying.

Peter was in the stable with Robyn, Tim, and Houdini. He looked up as Jenny walked in.

'I'm afraid he's sinking,' he said. 'We've done everything we can but he's not responding.'

Danni knelt by Houdini's side. The tears were streaming down her cheeks now. It was hard to believe that this was the same naughty little donkey who was always up to mischief. Always looking for a gate to open or a gap to squeeze himself through.

Very gently, Danni stroked Houdini's neck. A long shuddering sigh ran through the donkey's body. Danni gasped. She thought Houdini had gone.

Then a very strange thing happened. There was this weird noise — a mixture of wheezing, snorting, and soft braying. A gentle lulling sound of many donkeys. Then woolly heads and faces started looming over the half door of the stable as all the donkeys in the exercise yard came to see Houdini. They brayed in unison. 'Hee-Haw! Hee-Haw!' The stable was filled with the sound. Slowly, Houdini raised his head to listen. His eyes were clouded and his breathing dull, but he was responding to whatever his friends were telling him.

Danni snatched a handful of sweet smelling barley straw and offered it to him. But Houdini wasn't interested.

'Here! Try one of these!' Jenny handed Danni a gingernut biscuit.

Barnaby and Dolores poked their flea-bitten muzzles through the crowd. 'Ee-haw. Ee-haw,' they went.

And Houdini lifted his head to sniff at the biscuit. His lips started making those funny, pouting movements which donkeys make. That meant he was interested in the biscuit. Houdini wanted some food.

'Go and mix some bran and treacle,' said Jenny.

Then she turned her attention back to Houdini. The donkeys outside pushed their way past Danni as she opened the door and stood in the stable nodding their heads. It was almost as if they knew Houdini needed them. The donkeys all waited to encourage Houdini to live. They all wanted to be near him . . . to help him. If only they could.

It was incredible to watch. And at that moment Jenny realized just how important these donkeys were to her. Even if the factory did get built she would still have her donkeys. And they would always have a home at The Sanctuary.

The Sanctuary — Tuesday morning

The following morning Houdini was back on his feet. Thankfully, whatever it was that had upset the donkey had now passed, and he looked perky and alert.

No one was more pleased than Mrs Springer. Suddenly, she confessed that it might have been *her* who had accidentally fed Houdini with ragwort.

'It had such a pretty flower!' she said. 'I had no idea it could be so dangerous. I fed him some the other day as well. And I picked a bunch and used it to coax Houdini out of the Corner field. I'm terribly sorry,' she said, dabbing at her eyes with a tissue. 'I should have told you earlier,' she added. 'But I thought you'd all be so angry, and I felt so stupid at letting everyone down, especially with the sale of the field and everything.'

'You haven't let anyone down,' said Jenny flatly. 'But you should have told us about the ragwort straight away.'

'You are daft, mother,' said Robyn. She gave

her a hug. Robyn could see that she was really upset. Robyn had never seen her mother cry like that before.

'I'm useless,' complained Mrs Springer. 'I can't even look after a helpless donkey without messing it up.'

'But you weren't to know,' interrupted Danni. 'You weren't here when we talked about ragwort.'

'I know,' admitted Mrs Springer. 'And that makes it even worse. I was more interested in the shops than the donkeys. If I'd been here, then I would have known about the dangers.'

'Don't be too hard on yourself,' said Peter. 'You did a lot for the donkeys by trying to stop AUD buying that field. You helped to organize the protest and got more names on that petition than we ever hoped for.'

'And you were prepared to buy the field yourself,' remembered Jenny. 'If I hadn't dragged you out of the Town Hall you would have bought the Corner field to stop AUD getting their hands on it!'

'No! I would have bought it for The Sanctuary,' she said. Mrs Springer started sniffing again.

'You're my friends and I've really grown fond of these donkeys since I've been here. I know I wasn't too keen when I first arrived. But being here and sharing your problems has made me look at things differently.' She put her arms around Robyn. 'And I've never seen *you* happier,' she added stroking her daughter's long blonde hair. 'There's something about this place. Something very special. It's worth fighting for.'

Danni went all tingly when Mrs Springer said that. And it was true. The Sanctuary *was* worth fighting for.

Then Mrs Springer told them about the inspectors from the Ministry of Agriculture. When she stayed behind at the Town Hall after the field had been auctioned, Mrs Springer found out about the inspectors. They were coming down with other Council officials at two o'clock that afternoon to make a final inspection of the Corner field. Only then would AUD know if planning permission for their factory unit had been granted.

'They may have a field,' smiled Mrs Springer. 'But they don't have a factory yet.' Then she took out her car keys and unlocked the Mercedes.

'Where are you going?' asked Robyn. 'It's time to do the health checks now!'

Mrs Springer popped on her sunglasses and smiled sweetly. 'There was something in the shops which I saw the other day,' she said. Then she switched on the car's ignition and shot off out of the Farm.

Robyn couldn't believe it. Neither could any of the others. Tim arrived on his bike to find them all standing around with their mouths open — like goldfish.

And a short while later when the vet arrived to check on Houdini and re-dress Lucky's leg, they were still just standing there, gobsmacked with amazement.

Robyn looked embarrassed when Danni said out loud, 'How could she just shoot off like that after what she's just said? How could she go shopping again when she knows that the inspectors are coming?' Danni cast a quick glance at her mum.

'I think she's up to something,' mused Jenny.

Lucky's wound was only a surface scratch. The vet decided to leave the bandage off to let the air get to the wound.

She really was a very lucky donkey to have escaped that fall with such a minor injury.

Lucky was a very curious donkey. And after only twenty-four hours at The Sanctuary she was already eager to make donkey friends.

Lucky had been watching all the other donkeys out in the exercise yard. Shadow, Old Grey, and Jasper had already rubbed noses with her over the stable door. Captain had been giving her the eye from across the yard. This made Dolly jealous, and she nipped the old donkey on the rump each time he looked in Lucky's direction.

Lucky wanted company. And Houdini was lonely in the isolation stable. The vet said he should still be kept quiet for a day or two until he was fully recovered. Jenny thought it would be a good idea to put the two donkeys together. Houdini and Lucky thought it was brilliant. It was love at first sight. Unlike the feisty relationship between

Jenny Lester and Mr Pritchard the builder. Those two just didn't like each other at all.

They had just completed all the health checks when Mr Pritchard suddenly turned up in the Corner field.

'I suppose he's come to gloat,' muttered Danni.

But he hadn't. He didn't even look over towards The Sanctuary. Instead, he kept himself busy digging more holes. Mr Pritchard was digging holes and planting thin wooden canes.

'They'll never grow,' said Danni sarcastically. 'They've got no roots.'

Tim smiled and Jenny's face broke into a grin.

'I expect he's marking out the boundaries of the proposed factory unit for the inspectors to see,' surmised Jenny. 'It looks rather close to our fence, doesn't it?'

'I hope they don't let it go ahead,' said Danni. 'I hope something goes wrong at the last minute and the inspectors tell fishy Pilchard that he can't build the rotten factory.'

Jenny let out a big sigh and put an arm around Shadow's neck. The little donkey had nuzzled up closely for a cuddle. He seemed to sense that Jenny was upset about something. He looked into the Corner field and complained to the builder with a deafening 'Hee-Haaww!'

Mr Pritchard mumbled something under his breath and carried on digging his holes.

Tarbrooke

At two o'clock that afternoon, a procession of cars left Tarbrooke.

The first car was driven by James Ditchfield — Managing Director of Agrocure Universal Developments. The second car carried three inspectors from the Ministry of Agriculture. The third car held two local council officials. And a short distance behind, followed a white Mercedes.

The line of cars set off along the country road. Up and over the hill, past fields full of black and white cows, the procession headed for the Whistlewind Corner field to inspect the proposed factory site.

Tim was the first to spot the cars as they passed The Sanctuary and headed up the shady avenue of beech trees leading to Corner Cottage and the adjoining field.

He called to the others, not understanding why Mrs Springer, in the Mercedes, sailed along behind, and didn't drive into The Sanctuary.

'Why has she followed them?' asked Danni.

'What do you think she's up to, Robyn?' asked Jenny. 'Do you have any idea?'

Robyn didn't.

'Should we go and see?' suggested Tim.

'I don't think that's a good idea,' announced Peter. 'The council must be well aware of public feeling by now. They've seen the petition with all the signatures and they're here to do a job. We don't want to upset the apple cart and cause a scene. It might make us look like troublemakers.'

'But we can't just stand here and do nothing!' complained Danni.

'Sadly, I think we've got to,' sighed Jenny. 'But I've a feeling that Mrs Springer is about to do something on our behalf.'

They wandered into the grazing paddock to be nearer to the Corner field. They left the gate open and one by one most of the donkeys ambled in to join them. There was Daisy and Shadow. Dolly, Captain, Dixie, Old Grey, Blue, and Rosie. Jasper, Poppy, *and* Mr Barnaby and Dolores. The donkeys huddled in a big crowd, then fanned out along the fence and pointed their ears and eyes towards the group in the Corner field.

The clutch of inspectors studied a blueprint

drawing of the proposed factory site and discussed it in low tones. James Ditchfield and Mr Pritchard stood some distance away discussing building schedules. Mrs Springer joined them briefly, then wandered off on her own without discussing anything. She walked towards the canes planted in the field. There were several empty holes which Mr Pritchard had dug and not used. Mrs Springer hovered near these holes. Danni and the others could see her quite clearly. They waved, but Mrs Springer chose to ignore them.

She looked back at the inspectors, and Mr Pritchard who was busy talking to James Ditchfield. Then she reached into her pocket and dropped something into one of the holes. No one else in the Corner field saw her, but Danni and the others did.

'What's she doing?' said Tim, as Mrs Springer dropped something else into another hole.

'I've no idea,' said Robyn. 'But she's behaving really weird. She's got that look about her that she used to get when she was about to pull off a big business deal. I used to see it a lot when she was running her own business in London before she retired.'

Mrs Springer stood up and called to the inspectors. As they walked over to see what she wanted Mrs Springer pointed to one of the holes. Mr Pritchard and James Ditchfield also came over to see what was going on.

One of the inspectors reached into the hole and pulled out three muddy coins. He scrabbled around for a second try and found a few more. The coins were very old. The inspector held them on his open palm and brushed the earth away with his finger. The two other inspectors and the Council officials came to see what he had found.

'I saw something glinting in the bottom of the hole,' said Mrs Springer innocently, 'I thought it best to bring it to your attention. I thought it might be a lost ring or something.'

The inspectors seemed very excited about the unexpected find. The coins were Roman. And therefore very valuable.

'Are there any more?' asked a Council official. Mr Pritchard dug deeper into the hole but found nothing.

'There's some more here,' announced Mrs Springer. She had moved casually to the second hole and produced two more coins. The next minute, they seemed to be digging everywhere.

The chief inspector now held a pile of Roman coins in his hands and was speaking in hushed whispers to his colleagues. Finally he made an announcement.

'In view of this unexpected discovery, we have no alternative but to declare this plot as a site of historic interest.'

'What exactly does that mean?' asked Mrs Springer. Her eyes grew wide with make believe astonished wonder.

'It means,' continued the inspector, 'that we cannot possibly approve any plans to develop this plot.' He turned to James Ditchfield. 'That clearly means no factory,' he stated. 'I'm sorry. But what you *do* have is a field of obvious archaeological interest. I'm sure the local historical society would be delighted to arrange an organized dig on your behalf.'

James Ditchfield and Mr Pritchard looked crestfallen. Mrs Springer tried desperately not to give the game away and smile.

'Will it affect my property?' she asked innocently. 'Will I still be able to renovate Corner Cottage?'

The inspector told her that as long as she didn't make any external changes to the property, she could do anything she pleased. But the field would remain a field. Forever.

Suddenly the deathly silence which had fallen upon the group was shattered by an ear splitting bray. Shadow had thrown up his head to exercise his lungs. Little did he know it was a fanfare to The Sanctuary's triumph.

Everyone in Corner field turned to look. All the donkeys lined up at The Sanctuary fence began to bray in unison. It sounded like a very bad orchestra tuning their instruments.

Mrs Springer saw Robyn, Danni, Tim, Jenny, and Peter standing there looking anxious. This time she gave them a wave. She couldn't wait to give them the good news.

'Do you know them?' asked Mr Pritchard suspiciously.

'No!' lied Mrs Springer. 'But I'm sure I'll get to know them very well when I come down here to live. They look like really nice people.'

James Ditchfield and his builder stormed off to their car muttering under their breath about interfering busybodies and the luck of the devil. Mrs Springer smiled secretly to herself. It had been a good day's work.

The Sanctuary Kitchen — a little later

Mrs Springer explained everything. They all sat around the kitchen table hanging on to every word she said.

Robyn couldn't believe that her mother had

bought Corner Cottage at the auction. Neither could Jenny or the others.

'This is brilliant,' chuckled Danni. 'You mean after Mum stopped you from buying the Corner field, you went back into the auction room and bought the cottage.'

Mrs Springer nodded. 'I really like it here,' she said. 'And I know that Robyn does. I thought it would make the perfect weekend retreat. Besides,' she added, 'owning the property naturally gave me concern and interest over the proposed factory development. That's why the Council officials invited me along to the site inspection, so that I could see exactly what was going on.'

'And what exactly *were* you doing by Mr Pritchard's freshly dug holes?' asked Jenny.

'Planting a miracle,' she smiled. 'That's what was needed to save The Sanctuary and stop AUD from ever building here. I couldn't see one coming,' she added, 'so I thought I'd plant one!'

'*Plant one!*' They all looked puzzled.

Mrs Springer put a hand deep into her pocket and pulled out an old Roman coin. She slapped it down onto the pine tabletop for everyone to see.

'It's a Caesar quinarius,' she announced knowledgeably. 'They're quite unusual but not *that* rare. People dig them up all the time. Particularly around here. Did you know there was once a Roman fortress on the clifftop at Redsands?' she informed them matter-of-factly.

'Of course we know,' laughed Danni. 'Everyone knows. The tourists come to visit the ruins.'

'Who told you about them?' asked Robyn. She couldn't believe her mother would know anything about Roman ruins. Or old Roman coins come to that.

'The man in the antique shop told me,' grinned Mrs Springer. 'That's where these coins were found. Up in the ruins. I bought twelve and planted eleven of them in Mr Pritchard's funny little holes.'

'And when they saw them,' yelled Danni excitedly, 'the inspectors thought they'd been freshly dug up. That's mega brilliant.'

'No it's not,' grinned Mrs Springer. 'It's sneaky, I'll admit. But I merely planted them there and pointed them out. I paid for those coins fair and square. That's where I went this afternoon,' she informed them. 'It was the inspectors who jumped to the wrong conclusion, just like I did about this place. Anyway,' she added, 'there might be a whole Roman city underneath that field for all we know. It's possible. Houdini told me when we were having a chat.'

'Houdini!' laughed Robyn. 'So you've finally started talking to donkeys like the rest of us.'

Suddenly, Houdini bustled through the kitchen door into the room. The naughty donkey had unbolted the stable and was prancing around in the yard when he heard his name called.

Houdini made straight for the kitchen table and helped himself to a plateful of gingernuts. A jug of milk went flying before Danni was able to

grab him and lead him gently outside.

'So what will happen to the field now that they can't build the factory on it?' asked Danni.

'That's just one last detail I've got to sort out before we leave,' smiled Mrs Springer.

The Sanctuary — Wednesday morning

It was bright and early when the farrier came to check and file the donkeys' hoofs.

Lucky's hoofs were in desperate need of a pedicure. If they had grown any longer they would have started to give her real problems.

Danni, Tim, and Robyn picked the donkeys' hoofs clean before leading them to the farrier. They tethered each donkey in turn ready for Mr Barnes to give them the once over.

'There's a whole lot of talk in Tarbrooke,' said Mr Barnes, 'about Roman treasure buried in the Corner field. Half the town's coming out on a dig later this morning.'

'Does Mr Pritchard know?' asked Tim.

'It's nothing to do with him, apparently,' replied the farrier. 'Mr Ditchfield from AUD said they could dig up the whole ruddy field if they wanted to! He's washed his hands of it.'

'They won't find anything though, will they?' whispered Robyn.

'No!' said Danni. 'But it'll get rid of all that rotten ragwort. Perhaps we should be there to collect it all,' she thought suddenly. 'And make certain that it gets burned properly.'

'A good idea,' said Jenny. 'At least we'll get rid of that troublesome weed.'

The Corner field

Later that morning, an army of diggers arrived from Tarbrooke, determined to uncover a lost city of Rome. Mrs Springer went shopping, while spades, shovels, and trowels toiled at the earth.

Hours of digging, raking, and sifting harvested nothing from the soil. No city of Rome. No Roman artefacts. Not even one measly coin. But the possibility of treasure would always be there. The seed had been sown. The field was protected.

Danni, Tim, and Robyn ferried wheelbarrows full of ragwort to a bonfire in the far corner of the field. Wispy spirals of smoke rose into the late afternoon sky long after the last treasure hunter had left.

The sun was turning from yellow to a hazy burnt orange as Jenny brought drinks out to the paddock.

Danni, Tim, and Robyn sat on the fence sipping from their cans and congratulating themselves on a good day's work. Not a stalk of ragwort remained. The field was clear and safe.

'It will be rotten, going home tomorrow,' said Robyn. 'I've had such a great time.' She couldn't believe that a whole week had passed so quickly.

'But you'll be coming back,' cheered Danni. 'It's not as if you're going for good.'

Robyn still felt sad. 'It could take months before the cottage is finished,' she mumbled. 'And even then we'll only be coming for weekends and holidays.'

Danni and Tim exchanged sympathetic glances. They knew exactly what Robyn meant, neither of them could bear to be away from The Sanctuary for more than a day.

'You *will* write?' asked Robyn.

'And phone,' said Tim. 'We'll fill you in on all the news every week.'

'I want day by day accounts,' grinned Robyn. She was trying to sound cheerful. 'And I want to know as soon as anything happens with the field.' As luck would have it, she didn't have to wait very long at all.

The Sanctuary — 6p.m.

Mrs Springer had been out shopping for most of the day. But when she came back she didn't have any bags. That was unusual for Mrs Springer. She was always buying things. Lots of things. Today was different.

All that Mrs Springer returned with from her day out was an envelope. She handed it to Jenny across the kitchen table and beamed everyone a huge grin.

'What's this?' asked Jenny.

'Open it and see.' Mrs Springer stood behind Robyn and played with her long french braid.

'It's a present from me and Robyn.' Robyn pulled a face. She knew nothing about this.

Jenny opened the envelope and studied the contents. It was a legal document.

'I don't understand,' said Jenny. She looked surprised.

'It's a gift to The Sanctuary,' smiled Mrs Springer. 'From a grateful neighbour.'

The document was the land deed for the Corner field. Jenny handed it over for Peter to see. Mrs Springer had bought the field back from AUD. She had bought the deeds.

'At a fraction of the cost,' she added. 'Agrocure Universal Developments almost gave it away. Said they never want to set foot in that useless field again.'

'So it's ours,' exclaimed Danni excitedly. She nudged Tim. 'The Corner field is finally ours.'

'Not *ours*,' corrected Jenny with a grateful smile. 'It belongs to The Sanctuary, and the donkeys. Each and every one of them.'

'We got our miracle!' said Peter.

'We got Mrs Springer,' smiled Danni.

Mrs Springer laughed. 'Yawww. Yawww!'

Danni, Tim, and Robyn went hysterical. She sounded just like a donkey!